A PICTURE PERFECT AFFAIR

ALEXIS S. SHAYNE

The Hotwife Club - isbn # 978-1-59362-320-3
www.thehotwifeclub.com

EDITOR'S NOTES

The images that accompany these stories are not of real models but are generated with various Artificial Intelligence models. They are here to enhance your enjoyment of the story and are not intended to be 100% accurate depictions of the scenes and characters in this book. As a result you will notice a lack of consistency from image to image in terms of what the character, most often their faces, look like. It is not our intention to make you think we brought in models for a photo shoot here. In addition we included a couple of pictures in this book where the anatomy is slightly off just because we thought the image contained value in terms of enhancing the story. Overall the images included in this are not meant to literally illustrate the story and are here to add some interesting features to the book

You will also notice that none of the images are particularly explicit. The reason for that is twofold, first it is almost impossible to get quality explicit images from the AI art generators we used. Trust us, we tried. While there were a couple that produced overall accurate images it came at the expense of any subtlety. Secondly we understand and know our audience and you are all capable of generating far more explicit images in your own head than we could ever hope to do here as book editors. We are also mindful that someone somewhere down the line in a print production shop is going to see this and maybe not be 100% on board with what our notions of free speech include.

Now, that being said the story itself is one hundred percent from a human. The base of the story came from an experience related to a good friend of the author who in turn dramatized it to make for a nice, fun, bit of hotwife fiction.

The gift was unexpected. David, my husband of now twenty years, handed me a beautifully wrapped box, a mysterious glint in his eyes. Inside was a voucher for a boudoir photography session. I was skeptical. "If you wanted some dirty pictures of me all you had to do was make me an Old Fashioned and whip out your smartphone." I said, sounding a little irritated by the idea of going to a studio and getting my picture taken.

He chuckled, his hand snaking towards my waist. "Absolutely sure. I could do that, but I want to capture your beauty in a way that only someone else can see." His fingers brushed over the curve of my hip, sending shivers down my spine, something that had not been happening enough lately. This was way out of character for David, or at least way out of character for him recently.

I couldn't help but feel a flutter in my chest though, it was nice and sort of flattering to have this sort of attention from him, or at least to hear him say I was beautiful. Other than a few quirks about liking to watch me take a shower David had always been pretty reserved in the way he talks to me and very vanilla in the bedroom and honestly so was I. More concerning that we had wandered from a situation of vanilla, scheduled sex for the sake of it to one where we simply were not physical at all. Even a kiss goodnight seemed like more trouble to go to and we had gotten to a point where we rarely even sat next to each other at home. The most concerning thing about that situation though was that neither of us seemed concerned, sort of accepting it as a thing that happens to old married couples.

"Are you SURE you don't want to be there David?" I asked, hoping he would change his mind and come along. He shook his head saying "That would ruin the surprise of seeing the pictures." I had bought some new lingerie for the photo shoot, a nice three piece set with a robe to wear over it. I also picked up some matching nylons and a garter belt. I remembered early on in our relationship, before we got married, David told me he was a sucker for thigh highs and garter belts. I had worn them from time to time over the time we have been together and he always appreciated it, but I honestly did not like the way I looked in them. David was paying for this and I was getting the feeling that the pictures were more important to him than to me. But again, I was not really down with the idea of his not being there.

He leaned in, holding my gaze. "Amelia, I trust you. A little danger and risk might be good for us. It would be different for both of us if I was there looking over your shoulder, my presence might intimidate the photographer and they might not feel comfortable posing you with your husband there. The main thing is that I trust you, I always have. Whatever happens, remember that." His words held an undertone I couldn't quite decipher. He finished saying "Don't be afraid to be someone new."

I didn't quite get that, but I gave him a long kiss and a deep hug and went off to the car to go to the studio.

After a short trip and some time looking for parking I arrived at the space. I stepped into the studio, my heels clicking on the cool slate tiles. The room echoed with more than just the sound of my shoes; some very calming and sexy music was coming from a hidden sound system. Victorian style paintings hung from the walls featuring men and women in various states of undress and embrace. There was also a very large display of the photographer's work in the lobby and on the walls of the studio. Mostly the pictures were of women, but there were a few shots of couples in some very sexy poses, including one of a teller at the bank I went to and a man who I hoped was someone she was serious about. I wondered if she knew she was on display here, I wondered if she cared. I took some time to study the photographer's work and was very impressed. There were a few shots of people with my sort of body.

I was right in the middle of what we now call middle-aged. David and I had never had children, not because we planned it that way but it just never happened for us. We had talked about going to fertility clinics and trying a bunch of things but we had feared ending up with twins or triplets or other multiples that we would not be prepared to handle. Figuring that this was just life dictating a path for us we made our way alone, well not alone but with just each other and it all seemed fine.

The bottom line though was that my body did not show the signs that some women have of having children. My stomach was surprisingly toned and flat, with just a hint of softness around my middle. My breasts were perky and seemingly untouched by childbirth. No stretch marks lined my abdomen or

hips, and despite the occasional dark circles under my eyes, I had a vibrant sort of glow about me that could only come from never having to worry about taking care of kids. at least that's what I told myself. Who knows what other people thought. There were a couple of mirrors in the lobby of the studio, placed where they were so clients could get a good look at themselves before. I liked the way I looked, but was I sexy? I had no idea. Maybe this is what David was talking about when he said he wanted someone else to see the beauty in me.

The atmosphere of the studio was both tranquil and provocative at the same time, implying that I had walked into a sanctuary of art and sensuality. It was clear from the images hanging on the walls that this place only did boudoir photography; there were no family pictures or shots of youngsters, no pictures of grandma and grandpa in front of a fireplace, but there were one or two photos of more elderly models and couples. The pictures weren't risqué by any means, but they were sexy. Seeing the older couples in these images made me feel encouraged that these people had found some sexual fulfillment in what most people think is lost at a certain age. Nonetheless, the photos weren't overly explicit; they were simply alluring and in a way I envied them their enduring sexiness.

Suddenly, I snapped back to reality and heard a man's voice from behind me. "Hi, you must be Amelia," he said while extending his hand towards me, "My name is Rafael, welcome to my studio. I apologize for my assistant's absence. She is also my makeup artist and is currently getting everything ready for your shoot." He was tall with longer black hair tied into a ponytail, falling down towards the middle of his back. His tight jeans and black t-shirt showed off his sinewy swimmer-like build. As

he stood there before me, I couldn't help but notice his beautiful brown eyes and olive skin that hinted towards some sort of Latin background. But he had taken me by surprise since I didn't know the photographer was going to be a man, I had just assumed it would be a woman. My heart skipped a beat as I pulled my gym bag full of lingerie close to my chest, almost as if to shield myself from this stranger standing before me. I found myself cursing David for not coming with me.

I reached out and gave perhaps the weakest handshake in the history of handshakes. Rafael, for his part, did not seem offended. I imagine I was not the first woman to walk in here and be shocked that the photographer was a man. The name of the studio, Timeless Impressions, didn't even really suggest boudoir photography.

I wished I had taken the time to look up who I was seeing because not only was I not expecting a man I clearly was not ready for someone this handsome. As I visually took in his body my breathing became short and I fought to hide it so he wouldn't notice. Rafael broke the silence "This is usually the part where I give the client an opportunity to back out, clearly you were not expecting a man here, so if you feel uncomfortable please understand that you can leave and you will get a full refund. However if you stay and we start shooting I expect that the fee will be paid, although you can again leave any time you like." His tone was very businesslike and I took comfort in that. Clearly he had dealt with this sort of thing in the past.

"No, I mean, yes of course" I stammered. "I mean, of course I'll stay. I was looking forward to it!!" I lied, I wasn't looking forward to it but I was here and had a bag full of lingerie and I figured why the hell not. I guess this is what David meant about being someone new. I wondered if he knew the photographer was a man, he must have because doing research on this kind of thing was almost a religious experience to him. It's also possible he expected that I would leave, or call him or something and the one thing that is sort of the basis of my dealing with this kind of situation is to not give the other person what they are expecting. So if David expected that I would leave or ask him to come to my rescue, that is exactly the opposite of what I was going to do

"Excellent!" A smile spread across his lips, and I braced myself for the flood of compliments that were surely about to flow free, sort of the standard thing he probably gave all of his clients. "Amelia, you look stunning," Rafael said at last, his voice deep and smooth. "I'm honored to have the opportunity to capture your beauty on film."

I blushed a little at the compliment despite the fact that it sounded scripted. I felt good about myself and even in the casual jeans and a t-shirt I was wearing I liked what I saw when I looked back in the mirror. I didn't care if it was a false platitude. It was still nice to hear, but at the same time, I couldn't help but wonder what David meant by his words earlier. What new side of myself was I meant to explore? Was there something else going on beneath the surface or was I just overthinking this whole thing. David always told me how beautiful and sexy he thought I was and he also made a point of telling me that others felt the same way. He loved looking at my naked body and on a couple of occasions I caught him playing with himself as he watched me shower or get dressed. I suppose it never occurred to him to join me in the shower, or maybe he had and I rebuffed him because I was in a hurry, maybe he preferred watching. I have no idea?

David often teased me for overthinking things. If I took more than half a minute to pick out what I wanted at a restaurant, he would give me a hard time. If I asked the waiter to make alterations on my order, then David would make fun of me for wanting to customize my meal. He couldn't see that it had nothing to do with indecisiveness; rather, I knew precisely what I wanted and needed some time to form it or find something in the menu that was close enough.

Rafael guided me over to the makeup area, where a pretty young woman waited to make me look my best. As a redhead, I had particular difficulty finding the right hair and makeup combination. My fair skin and auburn-colored locks with a smattering of freckles could look too plain or too overdone: too much makeup and I looked like a cheap whore, while not enough and I looked like a little girl. I looked at the make-up artist again and smiled. What was her deal I thought to myself, does she work for this man or is there some sort of attachment. I felt a momentary feeling of jealousy which I quickly put out of my head. This woman had the power to make me look like just about anything and I was terrified she would make me look like a child. Maybe not a child, being in my forties meant an unmade up me looked sort of tired and worn out and I'm positive that's not the look my husband was wanting when he booked this session. Maybe he wanted the whore, I have no idea but at this point I wanted to look my best.

Being made up turned out to be a lot of fun! The makeup artist was truly skilled and had brought a lot of experience and knowledge to her craft, and she knew exactly what she was doing. She started with a light foundation that matched my skin tone perfectly, adding a hint of blush to give me a youthful glow. Next, she focused on my eyes, brushing a gorgeous golden eyeshadow onto my lids and outlining them with a subtle black liner. Mascara made my lashes stand out, and a touch of brow powder gave my eyebrows some definition. She asked me for suggestions but I left myself to her magic. After a few minutes, I started to relax and enjoy myself. The warm lights in the room made my skin glow, and the makeup emphasized my best features.

I became entranced by her gentle touch and found myself liking the way it felt. I often got my hair done, but never makeup and this entire process felt very intimate and was getting me in the mood for the session, which I imagine was something of the point. I hardly recognized myself with the carefully applied mascara, blush, and lipstick. My hair had been styled into loose waves that tumbled down my back, and the overall effect was stunning. Looking at my hair I made my one and only comment on her work "My husband likes my hair to have that freshly fucked look..." So she jumped in and messed up my hair a little more and got it looking pretty wild and out of control
I hadn't noticed Rafael coming into the room, as she worked her magic, he circled around us, capturing moments with his camera. "I love getting some behind the scenes shots, they look so natural and fun" he said. The way he moved was almost mesmerizing, and I found myself drawn to him in a way that I couldn't explain. He commented on the makeup and said I had

a natural MILF look, which made me blush at both the compliment and inappropriateness of it.

Rafael's assistant directed me to the dressing room, where I quickly changed into the lingerie set I had brought from home. The cool green silk bustier cami top had a string tie in the front and gently greeted my skin with a soft touch. I did not feel bound up in it and it accentuated my breasts and cleavage perfectly. I tied the top so I was comfortable with just enough squeeze to boost my boobs so they stood out and caught attention. They seemed to have a little release which I assumed was for clumsy men trying to tear their way to a woman's tits instead of undoing the string. Honestly I always liked keeping my top on during sex, maybe that was my own kink.

 With a grin I picked up the matching garter belt and stockings from their hanger and slid them on and ended with putting on the pair of fuck-me-pumps that I had also brought along with me. My reflection beamed back at me as I admired myself in the full length mirror. I felt very good about the way I looked and it all felt so natural that I almost walked out into the studio without putting on the panties (they go on last after the garter belt and nylons for those of you who do not know). I slid them on and then I grabbed the matching silk robe that was on a hanger in the dressing room. I started for the door to the studio when I remembered what was waiting on the other side, Rafael, a man, a man not my husband was about to see me in as intimate a getup as I had ever worn, and one that I specifically chose to elicit an arousal, just not one from a total stranger. I bounced this around in my head a bit and considered maybe not doing this, or asking for a normal photo-shoot instead of this sexy one, but then I figured Rafael was a professional and had seen plenty of women dressed like this so one more was not going to send him over the edge. Plus, this was me we were talking about, underneath all this silk and makeup was a semi-frumpy middle aged woman. Rafael looked like he didn't need any help in the ladies department, so out to the studio I walked.

As I stepped into the studio, Rafael's eyes widened in admiration. "You look absolutely amazing," he said, his voice low and husky.

His words and the way he was looking at me sent a shiver down my spine. Maybe I had read this wrong, maybe Rafael couldn't be trusted, maybe this was a bad idea. Maybe this was something he said to all his clients, like you wouldn't look at a woman who was paying you to photograph her and say "Jesus you look like absolute shit!"

Maybe, maybe, maybe ....

Maybe I didn't care. I did look amazing, at least I felt like I did. I had never felt so desirable before, and the feeling was intoxicating. My husband knew what this shoot was all about and while maybe he didn't know the photographer was a man maybe he did and didn't care. Maybe he was testing me to see what my limits might be, at what point I might call him and be angry for his having set me up. Maybe he did but one thing was certain; David had for SURE never seen me looking quite this good.

Rafael directed me to a couch and told me to get comfortable. He adjusted some lights. There was a fair amount of mood lighting in addition to the professional gear that surrounded me and it set the atmosphere in the room quite nicely. Candles and soft music in the background. a plush Victorian looking couch with fabric that felt warm and smooth against my skin. I breathed in deeply, to sort of steady myself and get relaxed. The room smelled of a sweet blend of raspberry and vanilla. A peaceful smell that was all at once soothing and arousing. He leaned me back on the couch and told me to relax, to not worry about the camera or about him, just to be in the moment and maybe close my eyes and think of the last time I felt truly sexy and wanted. I looked around the room and realized we were alone. "Where is your assistant?" I asked.

"

Marie? I think she was meeting her boyfriend somewhere and had to leave. No worries though, I have done this alone before

I don't really need the help. Unless you are concerned about us being alone together, then feel free to call your husband or ..."
"No!" I interrupted, not realizing I had shouted "This is fine, I was just wondering."

So the makeup artist had a boyfriend, and now I was alone in a very sexy looking room wearing almost nothing in front of a very sexy and maybe single man.

"But back to the question at hand, when was the last time you felt truly sexy and desired?" Rafael asked again as he he focused his camera, looking like he was finally going to take some pictures. My mind wandered back to a time, before marriage, before David even, when a man, a stranger actually, approached me at a bar where I was waiting for a friend to celebrate their birthday. The man, I don't remember his name and in fact I may never have known it, propositioned me. No romantic pretense, no beautiful poetic seduction, just a simple proposition. "You're the most beautiful woman I have ever seen and I must have you, tonight! Let me fuck your brains out and you'll thank me later."

I declined of course, but this man persisted trying every line in the history of bad pickup lines, and then he shocked me by offering me money. "How much do you want?" he asked "That's how much I want you, I'm not rich and I don't normally do this, but if money is what you need..." I was offended and told him to get lost, but he quickly apologized and said he was just taken up in the moment, that he wanted to be with me so bad that he would be willing to give me every dollar he had in his pocket to get me into a bedroom somewhere and, in his words "fuck you like you've never been fucked before."

I was a combination of shocked, offended and curious at the words that came out of my mouth. My first response was to make a joke of it "You have no idea how I've been fucked before" I said without looking at him and taking a sip of my drink. "How much?" I asked "What is it, what am I, worth to you?"

The man, whom I can barely even remember what he looked like, much less his name, said "I have about $500 in my pocket and I have access to another $500. So a thousand for an hour or an evening or whatever time you will give me."

Rafael's voice brought me back to the present. "You must have dug up quite a memory" he asked, his eyes dark with curiosity "You seem a little aroused, care to share?"

I hesitated before answering, unsure if I wanted to share that memory with him. But something about the way Rafael was looking at me made me want to share this intimate memory with him, just to see what his reaction might be. I am sure I had shared this with David at some point, at least I think I did.

"There was a time, before David, when a man offered me money to sleep with him," I said, feeling a bit embarrassed. Rafael's eyebrows shot up in surprise, but he didn't judge me, he didn't even seem shocked. Instead, he listened attentively as I recounted the memory. "So, what happened?" Rafael asked, he was now kneeling on the floor in front of me and was very close, maybe too close, but I did not push him away and instead adjusted myself on the couch and relaxed. Rafael liked the pose because he started looking at me through the camera as I talked and my mind went back to that bar with that man a long time ago.

"I looked that man in the eye and said, 'I'm not for sale, thank you. I appreciate the attention AND the offer, which is really generous, but I'm not a hooker and I don't fuck for money. Now, if you can get us a room in the next fifteen minutes, I'll show you the best impersonation of a whore that you've ever seen as long as you promise to fuck me like you paid for it." I paused in the story to get a beat on Rafael's reaction, which was sort of a raised eyebrow, maybe a bit of disbelief. So I looked him in the eye and under my breath I added "I may not fuck for money, but I do fuck for fun."

Rafael looked stunned at my admission. "What..." was all he could say as I continued. "He swept me out of the bar and into a room, it took more than fifteen minutes to get there, but soon we were making out in a hotel elevator, his hands were all over me and we were barely in the room when I ripped open his zipper, dropped to my knees and devoured his cock like it was my last meal."

He looked at me and said nothing, so I continued " I almost gagged on his cock giving him what was, I hope, the best blowjob of his life. I didn't let him cum though, I pushed him onto the bed and straddled him and fucked his brains out. Finally he flipped me onto my back and went at me like a jackhammer, it ended with him pulling out just in time and spraying his cum all over my stomach". I smiled recounting the end of the story. My friends occasionally make jokes about being with a thousand dollar a night hooker, for one brief moment long ago I sort of was one. I hadn't really thought about that night for a very long time and bringing it back up stirred me up, which I guess was Rafael's point even if he didn't expect such an explicit story. Rafael smiled, clearly impressed, and said "Well, you certainly know how to show a man a good time. That was quite an amazing story, it sounds like he was fucked like he had never been fucked before." He looked at me with some sense of longing, then got up from the ground and said "We have some pictures to take, that is some very nice lingerie, simple and sexy, trust me I have seen a lot of lingerie, most of it pretty cheap and trashy."

"Lingerie is lingerie" I said "It's the woman who makes it trashy.", I said trying to smile sexily and not sure what I was doing, or saying " I bought this for my husband to see, but you are the first man to see me in it."

"You're right about that, some women go from classy to trashy in a heartbeat and still manage to make it all look amazing." Rafael looked at me with appreciation and admiration, then said "I'm glad to be the first to see you in it then. You look beautiful and not trashy, but if you want to get trashy feel free, I excel at immortalizing trashy." He started to take some pictures, adjusting the lighting, adjusting me, trying to be professional, but I think my story got to him as I could see he was a little distracted. "So, is that how your husband fucks you? Like he owns you?"

"Do you ask all your clients that?" I replied, staring in what I hoped was a sultry manner back at him. "Nobody owns me, for your information, and my husband fucks me just fine." I was going for an indignant tone, but it came out sounding a little needy.

"Does he now" Rafael said as he went to lower the room lights a bit. This created an interesting atmosphere as the details of the surrounding room seemed to disappear and Rafael and I were left in a bubble of light.

This put me in an interesting head-space, the bubble of light surrounding us gave me a feeling that I was in a different universe. This was heading towards being like that night in that bar long ago. I was headed in a direction of doing something that was out of character for me, how far would I push this. I leaned back on the couch and let the robe I was wearing fall open exposing most of my body and the bustier and panty set I was wearing. I bent my knee so he could see the nylons and garters and put my hand on what my husband liked to call the negative

space, that exposed a bit of flesh between the top of the stockings and the bottom of the panties. "I think my husband might like something a little more... Explicit." and with that I started to slide my panties aside exposing myself to him.

Rafael's eyes widened "Amelia..." he said without really having an idea what he was meaning to say. He wanted to tell me to stop, but he didn't actually want me to stop. I had shaved for the occasion, leaving a small very nicely manicured patch above my pussy exposing it but with enough of a reminder that I am a woman and not a little girl. Being a ginger small bit of hair down there was barely visible. My husband loved it when I shaved because that man can eat pussy like a champ and he said he loved the full unfettered taste of me, but I didn't do it often because it was more work than I liked to put in down there. Shaving did make me feel sexier though and so I did it even if I didn't expect to expose myself.

I smiled and said "It's ok, I want you to see me. Take your time." I leaned back and let him take in every inch of my body. He moved closer, taking shots that highlighted the curves and shadows of my body. I felt a warmth in my chest as he admired me, it was like he was taking me into himself and transferring me into his camera. My nipples hardened and started to show through the top I was wearing, which I am sure made for good pictures because Rafael couldn't take his eyes off them. The camera clicked rapidly as he shot more pictures of me. The sound echoed in the confined studio space. After a few minutes, Rafael lowered his camera and stepped back, and our eyes met.

"You are spectacular," he said, voice low and reverent. "I've photographed a lot of women, and honestly, a lot of very beautiful women. But you have something going on inside that I can't describe." He continued snapping pictures, but his attention seemed divided. Whatever he was thinking was oozing out of his head and into me. I could feel the conflict building in him and burning into my skin like physical touch. I loved the attention and I wanted more.

"Honestly," Rafael murmured, "something about you... it's taking everything I have to stay professional." He hesitated for just a moment before continuing. "And just saying that means I've already crossed a line."

He wasn't the only one crossing lines, I was headed to my own line at full speed and with no way, or will to stop I started to put my foot on the gas. I was going to push myself across the goal line, but not all at once. Without hesitation, I began to move my body in a seductive way. My hips swayed back and forth as my hands trailed down my curves. Rafael's camera clicked away, trying to capture every inch of me on film. The thrill of being watched intensified as I continued to writhe in front of him, opening the robe and revealing more of myself to him. I thought of David watching me in the shower and wondered if Rafael felt the same way. Maybe that's why he became a photographer and why he has a specialty in boudoir photography. Rafael liked to watch and he must be getting off on this.

Rafael looked uncomfortable, both emotionally and physically. The bulge between his legs was growing by the second and was easy to see in his tight pants. Internally he was on fire in his head. I knew what he wanted, and I was more than willing to

give it to him, just like I gave it to that guy in the bar all those years ago.

I slid off my panties and then took off the robe, then I reached up to undo the bustier. I could have easily undone the top on my own using the clasp, but I decided this would be a good opportunity to bring Rafael in closer. "Could you help me get this off? I'm sure my husband wants to see my breasts in some of these shots."

Rafael stepped forward and untied the strings slowly, his fingers brushing against my skin as he did. I was so aware of each touch and the warmth of his body as he leaned in closer. I arched my back and let him move the straps of my top off my shoulders and then my arms. I felt exposed and vulnerable in front of him, but also powerful and beautiful. My nipples were now rock hard and pointing directly at him. He looked at me with hunger in his eyes that were devouring me whole, and I felt a thrill run through me.

I let my top fall to the floor, exposing my breasts to him but then coyly covered myself with my arms denying him too long of a look. He inhaled sharply, and I could tell he was trying very hard to keep his composure. Was this all an act, did he do this with everyone? I smiled and beckoned him closer, inviting him to touch me. "Put me where you want me..." I said softly. He hesitated for a moment before finally moving closer and grasping me gently by the arms, leaning me back onto the couch. His touch was soft and gentle, and I shivered slightly as I felt his skin against mine. He kept holding me by the arms, not restraining but just gently stroking, enjoying the sensation I suppose. We stayed like that for a few minutes, just enjoying the excitement of being close to one another as his stroke strayed from my arms and searched new places to touch. Finally, after what felt like an eternity, Rafael suddenly stepped back, and said "We need pictures of this, for your husband"

"Yes... for my husband..." I smiled. I had not been naked in front of someone who wasn't my husband or doctor for a very long time. Not since that night that I fucked a complete stranger fucked me like he owned me. I thought back to David walking me to my car a couple of hours previous and saying "Don't be afraid to be someone new." It was then that it dawned on me, David WANTED this to happen. He wanted to see me get horny and let go of my inhibitions. Maybe he thought this good looking man would get my juices flowing and I would run back home to fuck him senseless. Well, he was half right, my juices were indeed flowing but leaving was the last thing on my mind. I posed for Rafael, letting him capture my body in all it's glory, slowly changing poses and presenting myself to him for his entertainment and enjoyment. My curves and body were on full display as I playfully used my hands to alternately cover my breasts and my vagina. Rafael, seemingly inspired by my display furiously took more pictures, as he snapped away, I felt a liberation and freedom that I had never felt before. In those moments,

I was no longer someone's wife or girlfriend or whore but a powerful seductress in control of everything around her.
Rafael took a few steps back and clicked away with his camera while I posed and smiled, feeling more daring and liberated with each shot. I could feel his gaze on me and I loved it and it inspired me to get more daring with my poses. I could tell Rafael loved it too, I could see a bulge forming in his pants. He kept

yelling out encouragement like I was a supermodel, things like "Nice... Beautiful ... look away from the camera" I kept expecting him to yell out Blue Steel but that would have taken us out of the moment. I kept hearing David's voice "Don't be afraid to be someone new." and man was I ever someone new.

Rafael kept clicking away and he came back in to pose me again. His hands were warm. I could see sweat starting to bead a little on his brow. "Your husband will love this" he said as he leaned me back on the couch cushions and propped a pillow under my hips. His hands were dangerously close to my pussy and I could feel wetness growing between my legs. The room started to get the undeniable smell of sex, of sweat mixed with my own juices. Rafael was starting to sweat more too, I grabbed his hand away from the pillow and pushed it onto my crotch so he could feel the wetness for himself. "Do you think he will love this too?" I asked, pressing his hands against my wet crotch. I had no idea where this was coming from. This was like sexual improv where I was hoping for a Yes And moment. I was now in it and too far in to go back. "Do YOU like this?" I asked as I manipulated his hand and fingers in and around my moistened pussy. "Do you like how wet you make me? Do you make ALL of your clients wet?"

Rafael looked at me and I could see the desire in his eyes. He leaned forward and kissed me deeply. His one hand cupped the back of my neck while the other one began to rub me, his tongue was exploring my mouth and I did the same with his. There was no turning back now. I moaned with delight as he touched me, any guilt, hesitation or second thought I might have had disappeared as his fingers probed me. We were lost

in the moment, and we both knew where this was headed. We both wanted it.

I thought about David and what he had said to me. David wanted this to happen, he wanted me to break out of my shell and experience something new. At least I hoped he did because at this point neither me nor Rafael was going to stop. I pushed Rafael's head between my legs burying his face into my pussy. I moaned so loud that the sound bounced off the walls and came back to me like it was coming from someone else while Rafael's tongue darted in and out of me, licking my clit and going up and down my labia with his tongue, he started using his fingers on me at the same time and, whoa, this brought on some intense feelings of stimulation. It was gentle and rough at the same time, which I know sounds strange but this sensation was a new one for me, I couldn't believe that none of the men I had ever been with who tried to pleasure me with their mouths had ever so effectively used his tongue and fingers at the same time. This was a new territory for me and I was enjoying every moment of it. Rafael's tongue licked my aching clitoris with purpose while his fingers caressed the perimeter of my vulva, starting from the bottom and slowly exploring every part of it in what felt like an unpredictable pattern.

I was no longer the woman that I was when I walked in, I was someone new, someone confident, willing to explore herself and take risks. I was also the woman going over a cliff with no idea of what would come next. Rafael buried his face deeper into my crotch, his tongue and fingers stimulating me and sending electric shocks through my spine and into my head. I could feel the roughness of his face rubbing against my inner thigh, I gripped the pillows and moaned in rapture as Rafael ate me.

His tongue, his lips, his fingers, all of them working in unison to bring me to a climax. I was on the brink of exploding and I nearly jumped off the couch, I gripped the back of Rafael's head and nearly smothered him pushing him deeper between my legs. I instinctively clamped my legs together and thought that I might snap his neck with the intensity of my orgasm. My moans turned to a straight up scream that I am sure could be heard outside the building!

I gasped as I felt the satisfaction crashing over me and I clung onto Rafael as I felt my orgasm rip through my body. He stayed there, holding me by my hips until the last wave of ecstasy ended and my pussy stopped pulsing. I was covered in sweat, Rafael's face was soaked with a combination of my wetness and his own sweat. He held me gently, smiling and giving me a chance to catch my breath. I might have come, but he was not done

with me. I didn't WANT him to be done with me. His pants dropped to the floor and he nearly tore his shirt as he took it off. He grabbed my legs and gently spread them apart, leaned me back and positioned himself over me. He slipped himself inside of me with ease as we crashed together with a loud SLAP. His thrusts were deep and slow and I could feel every inch of him grunting with every stroke. He looked at me passionately alternately leaning back to take in the sight of me then lowering himself to kiss me. The newness of it, the feeling of a different cock entering me, it hit me like a ton of bricks. It was glorious. It was delicious and I didn't want it to end.

"Fuck me!" I screamed "Fuck me like you own me! Fuck me like you paid for me!" The intricate veins covering his cock felt like tree bark, hard and rough with a coarse texture. His fucking became more deliberate, he stopped his rhythmic banging and slowed things down, pulling his cock almost all the way out of

me only to slowly plunge it deeply back into me. He kept this up for a while and it was amazing. After a bit he started to pick up the pace a little and his inward jabs became more deliberate and forceful.

The couch shook with each plunge of Rafael's cock. He started pounding me harder and harder, pulling back and plunging into me ever deeper. Rafael manhandled me as he fucked me, squeezing my breasts, grabbing forcefully at my neck, leaning in to kiss me. He was working hard and sweating profusely, some of the beads dripped off his face and onto mine. It was dirty, it was exquisite and it was amazing. Tasting his salty sweat I wanted more. Soon The entire studio smelled like sex and sweat, a sour mix of pheromones and lust.

I was loving the pounding that Rafael was giving me, it was like he was driving me into the couch cushions and fucking me into submission. But I was a kid at Disneyland wanting to make sure they saw every ride and attraction, so I pushed him off of me and forcibly leaned him back. I took Rafael's cock into my mouth and swirled my tongue around it. It was salty and sweet, sweat and pre-cum with a small bit of me mixed in at the same time. I licked him clean then started to orally assault his cock with a sense of purpose.

The bulbous head of his cock filled my mouth and started finding its way down to my throat. I sucked so I could feel his shaft on the inside of my cheeks and could feel his bulging veins. I heard the gasp of breath escape my lips as I bobbed up and down his hard cock, almost gagging but taking him all in much to his delight.

I was in control of this man whom I had just met a scant few hours ago. Rafael wasn't just hard now, he was rock hard and he was moaning while at the same time begging for relief. I couldn't let that happen though, not yet. I pushed my tongue against the underside of his shaft, feeling every vein and bump with pleasure. I felt him start to twitch, his body tensing as he was preparing to explode in my mouth. I kept going, wanting him to enjoy every second of this experience. I felt the tip of his cock swell. He was close, but I wasn't going to let him finish like this.

He nearly screamed when I took his cock out of my mouth, he looked stunned and unbelieving. I flipped around so my ass was facing him "Fuck me from behind!" I exclaimed as I wondered who was actually talking now "Come all over my ass and save some for my tits!" Who was this talking, it sounded like my voice but I have never ever said anything remotley like that in my life! Rafael happily complied, grabbing my ass and lining up his cock with my pussy and easily shoved himself back into me. His dick felt like a hot rod of steel driving into me. The sensation was intense, I had already cum and normally I'm done when I cum, but his dick going back into me felt like it was finding new territory and taking care of some unfinished business. He grabbed onto my hips as he basically jackhammered my pussy with his dick trying to get himself off, his grunts getting louder and louder as the pounding intensified. I could feel him twitching inside of me, each thrust pushed in smoothly, gliding along my moist lips and coating himself, slick with joy, in my juices. Each penetration brought unexpected extra satisfaction. He started to moan louder and his thrusts become more aggressive as he got closer to coming, his moans turning into almost

violent grunts. He tried to pull out, but not in time and I felt a shot of cum go into me.

Rafael looked like he was in pain holding back the rest of his cum, then started to spray his cum all over my ass "Flip over" he yelled, I had forgotten I told him I wanted him to come on my tits. I rolled over just in time to get the last spray of his cum all over my chest with a little hitting my jaw and mouth. I wiped my chin with my finger, then licked them clean. I could taste the saltiness in his load and it was amazing, like a well-seasoned steak and I wished I had him come in my mouth. I slid my mouth over his penis to see if I could coax anymore out, but he was starting to get soft and was feeling sensitive, so instead I gently licked his cock and balls clean. It was more than he could take though and I didn't get a full taste. I took a moment to be amazed at how slutty I had become, I heard David in my head again "Don't be afraid to be someone new." I sure didn't recognize the person who was licking another man's cum off her fingers or had just let a complete stranger shoot half a load into her. Who was that person and more importantly who was the person who was going to go back to her husband.

I could feel the warm liquid running down my ass and legs as we both lay there panting and exhausted from the encounter. I swirled his cum on my tits around my nipples reveling in their sensitivity. We stayed like that for a few moments, just enjoying the moment, before he rolled off of me and on to the other side of the couch. We both lay there, exhausted from the experience, our bodies side-by-side and my heart still racing from the experience.

As I lay there, I felt content. I had just done something astonishing and it was a feeling that, much like the time with the man who was willing to pay me for sex all those years ago, I would never forget. But now I had to go home to my husband, my husband who had paid for this experience, and I had to figure out what, if anything I was going to tell him.

I got off the couch and went to fetch my clothing from the dressing room, but then I realized I was covered in cum and sweat (some of it my own) and who knows what else. As nicely appointed as Rafael's studio was, it did not seem to have a shower, but I did find some wipes and towels in the dressing room so I cleaned myself up as best I could and figured I would shower when I got home. I felt a little bad when I thought of David maybe deciding to wank to me taking a shower today and how ironic that might be. I mindlessly pulled my pants over my thigh highs and buttoned up my shirt before I realized I was not wearing a bra. Looking in the mirror I saw the reflection of a woman who had been freshly fucked, I went to fix my hair, but then figured why bother.

I went to give Rafael a hug goodbye only to find him standing in the middle of his studio, still naked and looking at his camera. There were several posed shots of me in them which with come color grading could look amazing, but then to my amazement there were some shots of us having sex. There was one of his head between my legs and my head tossed back, one of his cock in my mouth. Not very well composed and looking more like homemade porn than anything else, but you could see what was going on "I must have hit a timer when I set the camera down" he said. I never meant, I am going to delete these and I am only showing you them so you can see them being deleted.``

"Delete them," I said, trying to sound a little indignant, but in reality the pictures were getting me horny all over again. "But before you do that, please send me some copies so I can keep these memories." And something to show my husband, I thought in the back of my mind. I kissed Rafael goodbye and realized I would see him again to get prints that came with the package my husband bought.

What happened next was a case of what some people call "Post Nut Clarity". Driving home, a torrent of emotions coursed through me as I ran all the scenarios through my brain. What the hell did I just do? How would David react? Can our relationship withstand the weight of my choices? Did David set me up? Did David Set me up!!! Was this his plan all along? The questions swirled around in my head as I tried to make sense of my experience and come to terms with the feelings of betrayal and guilt that suddenly threatened to overwhelm me. My mind raced through these questions as I tried to figure out how I was going to explain what I had just done. Did I even need to say anything? Maybe the best play was to just lie through omission and say nothing. I mean, if David didn't ask and if he didn't suspect maybe this could just be my secret! That was never going to fly, at some point I was going to need to come clean (no pun intended) and admit what I did. I didn't recognize the person who was licking another man's cum off her fingers, but I knew that person was me and I also knew I had to be honest with my husband.

As I stepped through the front door and said hello to David, a sense of guilt mixed with satisfaction washed over me. On one hand, I had done something that was ethically questionable. But at the same time, I wasn't embarrassed or ashamed by it – a strange reaction that left me perplexed. I walked in the door and there was David at his home bar mixing himself a drink. "Hey, you're back! How did it go?" He slurred his words a bit so I knew this was not his first cocktail, maybe not even his second. He was smiling though and seemed happy to see me. I smiled meekly, still trying to figure out what to say. I sat at the bar across from him and smiled "got one of those for me?" He grinned, "Of course! What would you like?" he caught himself while he reached for a rocks glass "Who am I kidding, Old Fashioned right?"

"You know me too well, love" I replied "but maybe make it extra strong." I tried to search for the kindest words to explain what had happened at Rafael's studio. Kind, good words that would soften the blow echoed in my thoughts. In my head I was breaking it gently, easing into it and trying to soften the blow. In reality though, something else came out.

"I fucked the photographer!"

His face turned to stone and the only sound was an ice cube clicking against the bottom of a rocks glass. I continued with conviction, "He was smoking hot and irresistible and so was I in the lingerie I had bought for you to see me in. He didn't hold back once I gave him the okay and he was amazing. I'm sorry about it all, yet I'm not even a bit sorry."

David sat silent for a minute considering what he had just heard. I couldn't tell if he was smiling or frowning, his head was pointed down towards the drink he was making me and I couldn't say for sure, but whatever his expression he was certainly taking a moment to process.

"So, 'sorry, not sorry', is that what you're telling me?" David said, his voice measured as he looked up from the glass and up at me. "Were you someone else in that moment?" I hesitated and considered my response carefully. I had no clue who that person was getting a stranger's cock pushed into them in a photo studio, but I couldn't deny that it was me.

"I guess you can say that, but overall it all comes back to me."

David walked around the bar and moved next to me. He put his arm around my waist and for whatever reason I tensed up, not sure of where this was headed. I felt oddly aroused though as I felt a wetness returning between my legs. Was I getting turned on here, was Rafael's cum still finding it's way out of me? Was admitting my transgression turning me on?

David's breath tickled my ear as he whispered "Did you kiss him?", and I felt my heart stop. My mind raced with thoughts of what David might do, but before I could say anything, the word "Yes" slipped out from between my lips.

He kissed me, a warm, familiar wet juicy kiss that I had come to know over the years we had been together, and with that the dampness between my legs became a rush of moisture. I could feel it starting to escape me. David's hands moved quickly between my legs, feeling the wetness of my underwear. He took a firm grip on me, pressing his fingers deep into me as he asked, "Be honest with me, did you suck his cock?" The sensation of his fingertips on my skin sent a thrill through me and my sigh turned to a gasp, an instinctive response of surrender spilling from my lips as I croaked out the truth - "I did." His knowing fingers worked expertly, eliciting sensual moans that escaped from between my trembling lips as I succumbed to the probing of his strong hands.

My breath caught in my throat as David continued questioning me,"Where did he cum? Did he cum in your mouth?" His voice had a sharp edge, slicing through the air like a knife as if he was eliminating any opportunity for bullshit or other obfuscation. Nervously, I shifted under his gaze, not wanting to answer, knowing that this was going to change David and me as a couple, possibly forever. Taking a deep breath, I stuttered out the truth, but it sounded in my head like an excuse.

"Not directly" I gasped. David's fingers were tracing patterns along my skin that only he knew I liked, sending shivers down my spine. "He came on my breasts and some splashed in my face..." My sentences trailed off as soon as I began them, feeling embarrassed not just from the admission but from the thought that in the heat of that particular moment I was commanding that photographer to cum on my chest. But heat was rising within me as I recounted my encounter with Rafael. Thinking about the potential consequences, just like when I was at Rafael's studio, I decided to push things further.

"I licked some off my chin and decided to taste it, and I liked the taste so much I nearly swallowed his cock licking it clean." David looked intensely aroused, leaning forward and pressing his lips to mine, then throwing my head back like a vampire sinking its teeth into a victim's neck and kissing and playfully biting at my neck. He pulled away slightly and questioned me again, "Did he cum anywhere else?". Not wanting to look at him, but feeling powerless against the moment, I whispered: "He came inside me".

David's eyes widened at this and he pressed his body against mine as he moved his hand between my legs again, exploring me. His fingers moved slowly, deliberately, finding the sweetness within me was building back up. I gasped in surprise, feeling completely taken over by the sensations that were coursing through me. Finally, David looked me in the eye and asked one final question:

"Did you like it?".

I stared back, feeling embarrassed and aroused at the same time. My heart was pounding in my chest and my mind raced with the idea of what answer I should give. I could feel my face burning with shame and desire, but I answered honestly,

"No..." I said pausing for a bit of an effect figuring this might be a tipping point "I loved it."

David was silent, he handed me the drink he had made for me, as I took it he took my other hand and slid me off the barstool leading me towards the bedroom. My hair was a mess, bordering on that freshly fucked look that David loved so much, and my face was flush. What was going to happen next, other than a little playful spanking during sex when we were younger David had never raised a hand to me. What penalty would I play, was he going to make me pack a bag and get out. Maybe I shouldn't have admitted that I let Rafael cum in me, maybe someting else was a tipping point. I was afraid and almost trembling, not afraid for my physical safety but just afraid of what would happen next.

David stood me at the edge of the bed and started undressing. "Show me" he said "Show me and TELL me, everything he did to you." This was certainly not what I was expecting and I was unsure what I was supposed to do here. I decided I would get back in the headspace I was in the photo studio and just go with it. I Crawled onto the bed and got on my hands and knees, tempting him to join me. "You're wearing far too much clothing for that sort of demonstration."

Our lips collided as we writhed in passion, each of us desperate to make a connection. We made love with a fervor that felt like it could never have been possible before this moment. Every scandalous detail that came out of my mouth was like an aphrodisiac, the kind of filthy words you might say when you are living out a secret fantasy, role-playing a scenario that you might invent to spice up your sex life. Suddenly David slammed into me, and my body shuddered as I experienced another intense orgasm, my third for the day. Later I would find out there is actually a term for this; Reclamation Sex. David was taking me back, claiming me as his own. It was passionate and hot and glorious.

We laid in each other's arms afterwards and got our breath back. I was sore from all the pounding first from Rafael and now from David, but I felt amazing and satisfied in a way I find difficult to describe.

I looked over and David was smiling, covered in sweat and just getting his breath back. I loved this man, and what happened today was beyond comprehension, but in an odd way I think it needed to happen. As I looked at him smiling and seemingly satisfied and happy a thought crossed my mind and once again I found myself bluntly blurting out my inner thoughts.

"Did you pay that man, Rafael, did you pay him to fuck me?"

David looked at me, reaching out to brush my hair out of my face. "No" he said firmly " I did not pay him to fuck you." David rolled over and looked me in the eye " I didn't even realize the photographer was a man, I spoke with a woman on the phone. The studios portfolio was impressive and all of their clients raved about the experience, about how it made them feel sexy.

My hope was that the session with him would get you going and get you outside of yourself, I guess I was right."

I took a second to process what I was hearing. "So you didn't intend for me to have sex with him then?"

"Well" David said, considering his words looking for a way to sum up his own feelings "I guess I didn't know I wanted you to fuck someone else until you told me you did, does that make any sense?"

I stared back quietly at David considering what he said. On the surface it didn't make any sense but as I examined my own feelings, both now and back in the studio with Rafael, I began to understand. I didn't know how much I needed to have sex with a stranger until I did. Did I say need in my internal monologue? Did I mean want? Maybe I meant want and need? I looked back up at David and his feelings were a little clearer to me. "I get it, I think." was all I could muster knowing that this was not going to be the end of this and that more discussion was in store for us.

I put my head down on David's chest and he wrapped his arm around me. I was exhausted and I needed some sleep, but just as I drifted off I found myself saying "You know, I do need to go back to pick out what pictures I want prints of... maybe you should go with me and help me decide, or whatever." With that we drifted off to sleep knowing that our future as a couple had dramatically changed and where it went was up to us.

ALEXIS S. SHAYNE

A PICTURE PERFECT AFFAIR

ABOUT THE AUTHOR

*B*EFORE ONLYFANS MADE MILFS a commodity, Alexis S. Shayne was a seasoned player in the world of sex work, juggling roles as a provider, model, psychologist, mentor, and yes, a mother. Her foray into the world of escorting granted her an intimate look into the myriad desires of men and women, knowledge she now channels into her storytelling. As she transitioned from whispered encounters under the sheets to the writer's desk, her writing took a witty, candid form. Although categorized as fiction, much of Alexis' work stem from her own rich tapestry of experiences or those shared with her by others. Through her prose, she explores the quirks of human desires, the ironies wrapped in intimacy, and the often blurry divide between love and lust.

the HOTWIFE CLUB

Cool stuff for your favorite Hotwife or Vixen

www.thehotwifeclub.com

www.ingramcontent.com/pod-product-compliance
Lightning Source LLC
Chambersburg PA
CBHW051558120626
46551CB00013B/1568